Nate the Great
and the
PHONY CLUE

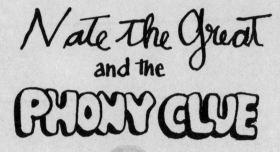

this book belongs to

Andy C.

Nate the Great
and the
PHONY CLUE

by

Marjorie
Weinman
Sharmat

illustrated by Marc Simont

A Yearling Book

Published by
Bantam Doubleday Dell Books for Young Readers
a division of
Random House, Inc.
1540 Broadway
New York, New York 10036

ISBN: 0-440-46300-9

Reprinted by arrangement with
Coward, McCann & Geoghegan, Inc.

Printed in the United States of America

March 1985

37 39 40 38 36
CWO

For 133 Dartmouth Street

I, Nate the Great,
am a great detective.
I have just solved a big case.
It did not look
like a big case when
it started this morning.

My dog, Sludge, and I
were running
around the block
for exercise.
We ran past Annie
and her dog, Fang.
We ran past Rosamond
and three of her cats.

We ran past Finley
and his friend Pip.
We ran home.
I saw a piece of paper
on my doorstep.
I picked it up.
It was thin paper.
VITA was printed in ink on it.
The paper was torn off
around VITA.

What did it mean?

I got my dictionary.

I looked up "vita."

I found that "vita" could be

the start of a word.

"Vita" could be the start of
"vitamin" A, B_1, B_2, B_6, B_{12},
C, D, E, G, H, K, or P.
Or "vita" could be the middle
or end of a word.

It could even be
part of a long message.
The mystery got bigger
as I thought about it.
I, Nate the Great, knew
there was a missing piece or pieces
to the paper.
Who or what had torn them?
I let Sludge
sniff the piece of paper.
"We will look for the pieces,"
I said.
I, Nate the Great, thought.
Who or what tears paper?
Of course! Rosamond's cats.
Four cats. Sixteen claws.

Sixteen claws could tear
a lot.
I wrote a note to my mother.
Then I tore it into pieces.
Then I fitted the pieces
back together.

I put a pancake in my pocket.
Then Sludge and I went
to Rosamond's house.
Rosamond was outside

with three of her cats.

Rosamond looked strange.

But she always looks strange.

"Hello," I said. "Did you

leave a note on my doorstep
this morning?
Did your cats tear it?"
"No," Rosamond said. "I did not
leave a note on your doorstep."
I looked at her cats.
They look strange, too.

"My cats have been with me
all morning," Rosamond said.
"Except Big Hex. Big Hex
spent the morning
in his favorite tree."
"Big Hex tears paper," I said.
"Yes," Rosamond said.
"Big Hex tears, rips,
scratches, shreds, cuts,
slits, and slashes."
"I see," I said.
"Did Big Hex tear,
rip, scratch, shred, cut,
slit, or slash
a piece of paper today?"
"Ask him," Rosamond said.

I looked up.
I saw Big Hex
sitting on a branch
of the tree.
I, Nate the Great,
was in luck.
I saw a piece of paper
stuck on a twig
close to Big Hex.
Too close.

I reached into my pocket
and pulled out the pancake.
I threw it to the ground.
Big Hex jumped down and started
to eat the pancake.
I reached up and grabbed
the piece of paper.
Now I had two pieces.
I put them together.
"They fit!" I said.
"It *is* a message. Look.
Now the paper says
INVITATION
COME TO MY HOUSE AT THREE.
'Vita' was part of 'invitation.' "

"You solved the case,"
Rosamond said.

"No," I said. "There is still a
missing piece with a name on it."

"What name?" Rosamond asked.

"The name of the person who
wrote the invitation," I said.

"I, Nate the Great,
will find the missing piece.
I will find it before three."

I started to leave.

"Wait," Rosamond said.

"Big Hex wants to thank you
for the pancake."
"How does Big Hex thank?"
I asked.
"With a kiss," Rosamond said.
I, Nate the Great, did not
want to be kissed by anyone
who tears, rips, scratches,
shreds, cuts,
slits, and slashes.
"No thanks for the thanks,"
I said.
Sludge and I ran home.
It was time for lunch.
I made some pancakes.
I gave Sludge a bone.

We ate and thought.

Where was the missing piece
with the name on it?

I, Nate the Great, had to know
by three o' clock.

Sludge and I started out again.

I saw Annie and her dog, Fang,

coming down the street.

They were with Finley and Pip.

Pip does not say much.

Finley says too much.

"I, Nate the Great, am looking
for a piece of paper
with a name on it," I said.

"Why are you great?" Finley asked.

"I solve cases," I said.

"I find and I find out."

"Why don't you find the piece
of paper?" Finley asked.

"Nate the Great will find it,"
Annie said.

"Ha!" Finley said.

"Maybe he's great;
maybe he's not."

Pip said nothing.

Finley and Pip walked away.

Sludge turned and followed them.

I turned and followed Sludge.

Annie and Fang turned
and followed me.

I saw Finley drop a piece

of paper into the sewer
and walk away.
I looked into the sewer.
I did not like
the way it looked.

But the paper was there.
It could be the missing piece.
How could I get the paper out?
I, Nate the Great, needed
something long and sharp.
I saw something long and sharp
beside me.
Fang's teeth.

Then I had another idea.
I looked
down at the paper again.
It looked blank.
"The print must be on the side
that is facing down," I said.
"We must wait."

"Wait for what?" Annie asked.
"Wait for the water in the sewer
to make the paper very wet.
The invitation is printed
in ink on thin paper.
When paper is thin and
the printing on it is dark,
water can make the printing
show on the other side.
Then we can read the name."
"But won't the printing
look backwards?" Annie asked.
"Yes, but nothing is perfect.
I, Nate the Great, say that
nothing is perfect."
The paper was getting

wetter and wetter.

I saw some printing on it.

I saw . . . .

"Phony clue!" I said.

I, Nate the Great, was mad.

I had never had

a phony clue before.

I did not know what to do.

I could not find the missing piece.

I looked at the pieces in my hand.

I, Nate the Great, thought.

Then I said, "I am looking

at what I have.

Perhaps I should look

at what I do not have."

"How can you do that,"

Annie asked,

"when you do not have it?"

"Look!" I said. "When I put

the two pieces together,

the empty space that is left

is shaped like a boat.

So the missing piece
is shaped like a boat.
I, Nate the Great, will
look for a paper boat."
"What if you can't find it
before three o'clock?"
Annie asked.
"Then I am sunk," I said.
Sludge and I walked and thought.

I, Nate the Great,
had seen a boat today.
But where?
It was not
on the Atlantic Ocean.
It was not
on the Pacific Ocean.
It was on a paper ocean.
Sludge and I ran
to the paper ocean.
The paper boat was there.
I fitted my pieces
of the invitation
around it.

Aha! They fitted. The paper boat
was the missing piece.
The paper boat was . . . blank.
It did not tell me anything.
Or did it?
Now I knew that someone
wrote an invitation to me
and did *not* sign it.
The same someone tore
the invitation into pieces
and left one piece
on my doorstep
and put one piece in the tree
and pasted one piece
on the paper ocean.
Someone did not think that

I, Nate the Great, could find out
who the someone was.
Someone was testing me.
I looked at the paper boat
on the paper water.
Hmmm. Paper and water.
I had just seen paper in water.
The phony clue in the sewer.
I, Nate the Great, had an idea.
Sludge and I ran home.
I filled my sink with water.
I took the two pieces
of the invitation
and turned them over
and put them in the water.
Now the printing on them

was wet and backwards.
I, Nate the Great, looked
at the printing.
There was that funny E, again.
The printing was the same
as the printing on the
"phony clue."

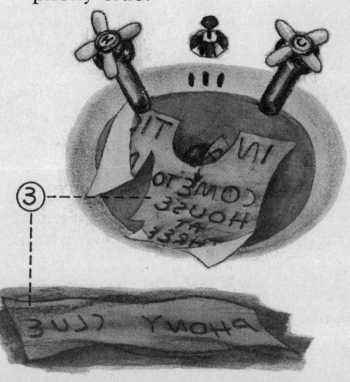

I, Nate the Great,

knew the case was solved.

It was not yet three o'clock.

This was an invitation

I wanted to answer exactly on time.

Sludge and I

ran around the block

and around the block

until it was three o'clock.

Then we went to Finley's house.

Finley was with Pip.

Pip did not say anything.

"It is three o'clock," I said.

"And I, Nate the Great, am here.

I have answered

your invitation, Finley."

Finley gulped.

"I, Nate the Great, say
there is no such thing
as a phony clue.
The printing on your phony clue
is the same as the printing
on the invitation.
You wrote the invitation.
You tore it into pieces."

Finley gulped again.

Pip opened his mouth.
At last he had
something to say.

"I win!" he said. "I told
Finley that you would
solve the case

by three o'clock."

"I lose," Finley said.

"You *are* a great detective."

"Thank you," I said.

I, Nate the Great, felt great.

I was glad the case was over.

Sludge and I started to run.

We ran past Annie and Fang.

"I solved the case!" I said.

"I knew you would!" Annie said.
Annie and Fang started to run
beside us.

We all ran home
for pancakes
and bones.